Little Brother Moose

To the One who created all. — *James Kasperson*

To my parents, Jack and Lucille Welton, who have given me unconditional love and encouraged me to pursue my dream of being an artist. — *Karlyn Holman*

ISBN paperback 1-883220-33-5
hardback 1-883220-34-3

Published by DAWN Publications
P.O. Box 2010
Nevada City, CA 95959
800-545-7475

nature@dawnpub.com

Printed in Hong Kong

13 12 11 10 9 8 7 6 5
First Edition

Designed by LeeAnn Brook
Type style is Walbaum
Illustrations are in transparent watercolor with white ink.

LITTLE BROTHER MOOSE

James Kasperson
Illustrations by Karlyn Holman

DAWN PUBLICATIONS

Long ago, the Algonquin Indians lived with many animals in the woods. They thought of all parts of the earth and all animals as family. They named the moose, "Moss" or "Moswa," which meant twig-eater in their language. Today moose still live in the northern regions of the world. This is the story of a moose.

At sunrise Moss took a drink from the big lake. He had traveled next to ice covered water for days. Today the lake greeted him with open water. He drank the cold, clean water and then stood still.

Moss listened. To the north. The east. Then his ears twitched to the south. Laughter. The laughter of a small stream as it reached the lake after a long spring journey.

Moss stepped into the laughing stream. He smelled the musty odor of the bog carried in its water. He listened again, this time to a small voice within him. This voice did not speak through his ears alone but through his eyes, his nose, his mouth, his whole body.

He first heard the voice last year when he still ran with his mother, but it was more than her voice alone. It carried on the wind, spoke through the seasons, shouted out in hunger, and signaled through the movement of an approaching wolf.

Moss listened to this voice when he made his decisions.

The voice spoke of the bog. "Come home, little brother."

Moss followed the river through the morning. Wet snowflakes began to fall. He crossed a meadow and stopped to munch on willow tips. Soon his meals would be the green shoots of spring.

He noticed a new smell.

Danger. Bear. Upstream.

The voice was speaking again.

"Leave the river."

Moss climbed the riverbank. He heard the sound of another river over a hill.
This river roared, as if filled with spring water pounding against rocks.
He climbed to see the new river.

The river was unlike any that he had seen before.
It was full of speed and power.

The voice whispered, “Danger, return to the creek.”
But the river called loudly, “Follow me!”

Moss stayed high on the ridge and followed the river.
He forgot about the bog. He chased excitement. A new smell.
A new movement. A new river.

After a while the roar stopped. The river looked different.
There was no movement. Moss approached the river cautiously.
He stepped to enter the river and stood on its surface. This was a hard river.

Branngh. Branngh.

A creature with wild shining eyes passed by him suddenly. It bellowed louder than any moose he had ever heard.

Moss ran.

Moss was away from the danger, but he didn't stop running.
Although the smell of the creature still burned his nose,
it was a new smell. It was exciting.
It called him onward.

By late afternoon Moss was still walking. His stomach told him it was time to eat but he could find no willow tips. There were no laughing streams to follow. Only hard rivers. He followed a hard river until it ended between two cliffs. He stood the night there.

At daybreak, he was
chased by another
wild-eyed creature.
He ran between the many
cliffs of this new world.
The roar of the hard rivers
was all around him.

Moss stopped running in a clearing. It was filled with wild-eyed creatures.
Their eyes were dark and they all stood still.
He quietly walked past the sleeping creatures.

Moss was hungry and thirsty.
He listened for the sound of water.
There it was. A faint hollow trickle.
Moss followed the sound.
It was coming from
a hole near his feet.
He lowered his nose near the hole.
He saw water flowing a few
feet beneath him. It was a stream.
Out of reach. Behind a grate.

He looked for food. He found some trees with
vines connecting them. They had no leaves
or buds, only spikes that rose beyond his
reach. He nibbled at one.
The metallic taste
sent him down
the alley.

He smelled food in the air. It was woody and pungent like cedar. The odor became stronger as he walked. He could see stacks of large brown mushrooms with steam rising from them.

He couldn't reach them.

It was time to go home. Moss had to find the bog.
Where was the voice? He heard nothing but the roar of the activity surrounding him.
He smelled nothing familiar. He saw nothing that looked like home.

He spent a day and a night by some small trees.
He nibbled on the trees but they
were not enough.

Everything around Moss was constantly changing. New creatures approached him. They stood away from him and pointed.

Moss was surrounded by colors, shapes, smells and sounds that were unknown in the bog. He was alone and could not hear the voice. He was frightened.

As evening came Moss was less afraid. He was
getting used to the noise and movement of this busy world.
But it was not his world. He'd had enough of its excitement.
He wanted to go home if he could find the way.
Where was the voice?

At dawn he listened. Honk. Honk. There was motion above.
A V-shape was flying through the dawn. Honk. Honk. Geese.
They were calling to him. He followed.
He heard the voice in their calls.

The geese flew out of sight.
He traveled in the direction
that they flew.

Just as he began to feel lost again, he listened.
Honk. Honk. Another flock. They were low.
He reached out his long neck to touch them.
Then, on the breeze, he caught a whiff.

The bog. He could smell his home on
the geese.

The voice was speaking again. "I am here. Follow me. Come home."

Moss walked for the whole day. The busy world was now behind him.
The geese kept coming. They pointed the way.

By evening Moss was far from the last hard river. He found some willow tips and ate. Then he heard it. Laughter. The laughter of a small stream.

He leapt in. The voice spoke clearly now. The feel of the water, its gentle laughter, and the smell of the bog just upstream. They all said one thing, "Welcome home, little brother."

The event of a moose entering town is quite common to northern communities in moose range. They enter towns for a variety of reasons, including illness. Naturalists speculate that young apparently healthy males enter town for a different reason: curiosity.

Geese migrate every spring and fall punctuating the seasons with their haunting call. In many ancient cultures geese were considered divine messengers.

Listening is one of the first things that many creatures do. Even before birth we hear the comforting thump of our mother's heart. Animals listen to the world around them in order to survive. Newborn animals and birds listen for the approach of their parents with food. They follow the call of their parents when danger is near. Rabbits and deer have only their senses and their feet to insure their safety. Fish listen for the sounds of a wounded minnow in order to find their next meal. Bats navigate through the darkness by hearing echoes as they bounce off objects.

Listening is not just an activity that we do with our ears. It is an attitude of our whole being. To listen is to be in relationship with the world around us. Through listening we become aware of who we are. We also become aware of the magnitude and power of life around us.

People have listened to the earth throughout time and have seen the earth as part of their family. St. Francis, a twelfth century monk, spoke to the birds of the field and to the wolves in the caves outside of Assisi. He called the sun "brother" and the moon "sister." Shrines are built in the mountains of Japan to the spirits of the water and the trees. In many tribes, the American Indians have called the animals around them "little brothers."

The voice of the earth is the voice of life for our world. It dwells within us and around us. As human beings we are surrounded with many sounds, the sounds of our society. Like the little brothers of the earth we, too, need to listen through the noise, to the quiet voice of life.

About the Author and Illustrator

DON ALBRECHT

The rivers, lakes and wetlands of northern Minnesota and Ontario were the places that James Kasperson realized his love for the earth. He is an ordained minister and has served rural congregations and outdoor ministries in northern Minnesota, Wisconsin and Alaska. He is also a musician, poet, and storyteller, and leads environmental and spiritual workshops for families, teachers and children throughout the Upper Midwest. In his first book, **More Teaching Kids to Love the Earth**, published by Pfeifer-Hamilton in 1994, he shares stories of being in relationship with the earth. **Little Brother Moose** is his first children's book.

Karlyn Holman's watercolors reflect a special exuberance for her native area of Lake Superior. Karlyn has an M.A. in art from the University of Wisconsin and has taught at the college level for twelve years. She is a full-time artist and has owned her own studio-gallery since 1968. She teaches high-spirited watercolor workshops throughout the world. This is the second book that she has illustrated.

Acknowledgments

I thank my family, Jan, Kaleb, Siri, and Soren, for their support and patience with my writing. They have each made sacrifices. I also thank the other people who have supported me and believed in this project, Karlyn Holman, Marina Lachecki and Mary Rice. Their encouragement and enthusiasm were essential to my on-going effort in this work. I am grateful to Bob Rinzler and Dawn Publications for their belief in this project. I especially appreciate the wise and gentle guidance of my editor, Glenn Hovemann. His insight, joy and creativity have added much to this book. — James Kasperson

I thank my husband Gary for his encouragement. I thank James Kasperson for his faith in my ability as an illustrator. I also thank my friend Kelly Randolph and my daughter Renee Holman for providing invaluable moose references. I thank Bob Rinzler and LeeAnn Brook for their invaluable help in guiding me through this adventure. — Karlyn Holman

Other distinctive nature awareness books from Dawn Publications

Stickeen, John Muir and the Brave Little Dog by John Muir as retold by Donnell Rubay. In this classic true story, the relationship between the great naturalist and a small dog is changed forever by their adventure on a glacier in Alaska.

Motherlove by Virginia Kroll. The love of a mother for her young, it is said, is the closest echo of love divine. This book is a celebration of motherlove—in both animals and humans.

With Love, to Earth's Endangered Peoples by Virginia Kroll. All over the world, groups of people, like species of animals, are endangered. This book portrays several such peoples, with love. (Teacher's Guide available.)

Lifetimes by David Rice, introduces some of nature's longest, shortest, and most unusual lifetimes, and what they have to teach us. This book teaches, but it also goes right to the heart. (Teacher's Guide available.)

A Drop Around the World by Barbara Shaw McKinney, follows a single drop of water on its worldwide water cycle journey, inspiring respect for water's unique role on Earth. (Teacher's Guide available.)

A Swim through the Sea by Kristin Joy Pratt. This young author-illustrator's alphabet format book uses delightful alliterative verse to introduce the ocean habitat. Similar habitat-based books by this author: *A Walk in the Rainforest* and *A Fly in the Sky* aid in inspiring children with an appreciation of all life on Earth. (Teacher's Guides available.)

Dawn Publications is dedicated to inspiring in children a deeper understanding and appreciation for all life on Earth. For a copy of our catalog please call 800-545-7475. Please also visit our web site at www.dawnpub.com.